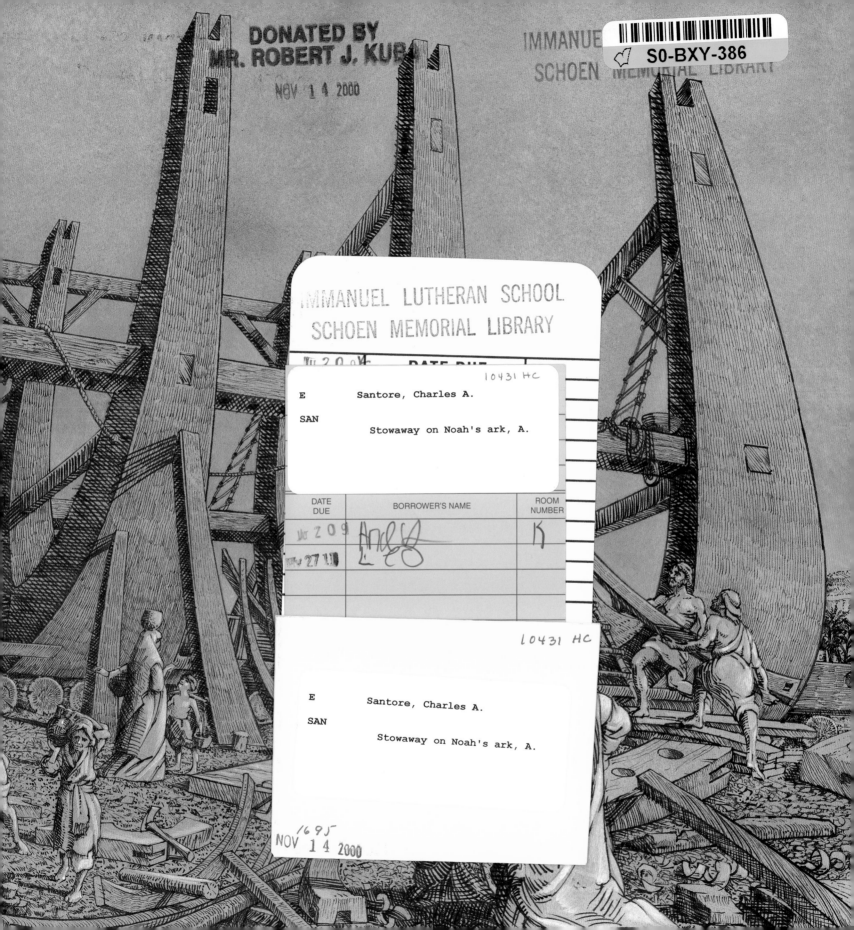

For my brother, Joe Hart
–C.S.

Copyright © 2000 by Charles Santore. All rights reserved under International and Pan-American
Copyright Conventions. Published in the United States by Random House, Inc., New York, and
simultaneously in Canada by Random House of Canada Limited, Toronto.

www.randomhouse.com/kids

Library of Congress Cataloging-in-Publication Data
Santore, Charles. A stowaway on Noah's Ark / written and illustrated by Charles Santore.   p.   cm.
SUMMARY: Not having been chosen by Noah, Achbar the mouse stows away on the ark and tries not to
be discovered while he and the other animals await the end of the flood.
ISBN 0-679-88820-9 (trade). — ISBN 0-679-98820-3 (lib. bdg.)   [1. Noah's ark—Fiction.
2. Mice—Fiction.   3. Animals—Fiction.   4. Noah (Biblical figure)—Fiction.]
I. Title.   PZ7.S2383St   2000   [Fic]—dc21   98-23272

Printed in Hong Kong   October 2000   10 9 8 7 6 5 4 3 2 1

RANDOM HOUSE and colophon are registered trademarks of Random House, Inc.

A Stowaway on Noah's Ark

written and illustrated by

Charles Santore

Random House New York

Once, in an ancient and troubled time, there lived a kindly old man who spoke to the sky.

One day, the sky spoke back. "The people have become wicked and evil," said a mighty voice. "I will send a great flood to destroy this wicked world and wash the land clean. All living things shall be wiped from the earth. You and your family alone will survive. Build a great ark of cypress wood to shelter creatures both large and small. Choose two of each animal. This is the task I set before you."

The old man obeyed. With the help of his wife, his three sons, and his sons' wives, he began building an enormous ark of sturdy timber.

After many years, the giant vessel was finally finished, and the
old man sealed the seams with pitch inside and out.

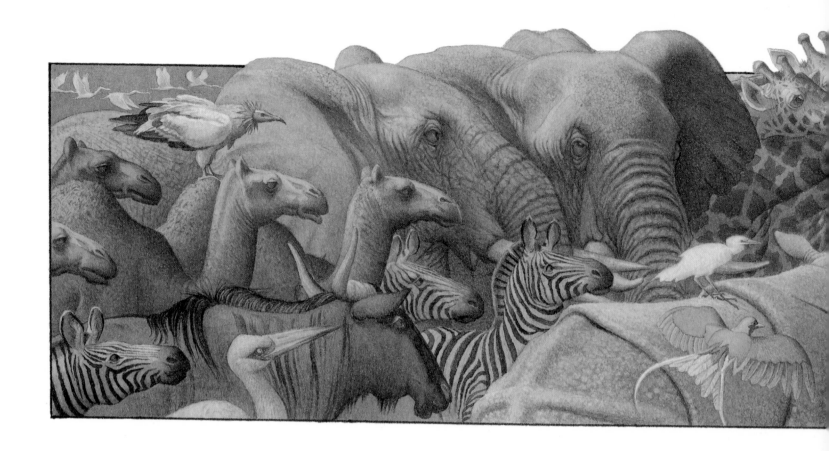

Then the old man gathered all the animals of the world
together. He told them what the voice in the sky had foretold
of the coming disaster, about the terrible flood that would cover
the earth and all living things. And he began selecting two of
every creature to join him on the ark, just as the voice had
commanded.

Little Achbar was there in the valley when the animals were
selected, but he was not chosen. Two mice had already been
picked for the voyage. In the dusty maze of hoofs, paws, and
general confusion, he had been overlooked.

Disappointed, Achbar watched as those who had been chosen
formed a column, two by two, which stretched across the plain
as far as he could see. When the line of animals finally began to
move, Achbar followed along out of curiosity.

After many days of walking, he saw the ark for the first time, looming like a mountain in the distance. It was enormous. Achbar had never seen anything so big. He watched in wonder as the cargo of walking, crawling, and flying beasts slowly filled the ark.

Meanwhile, the midday sky was growing dark. Achbar heard
the low rumble of distant thunder and it frightened him. A great
storm was surely coming, just as the old man had said.

Achbar thought of the flood and shuddered. At that moment,
lightning flashed close by and thunder shook the earth. Achbar
decided right then that he would not be left behind.

The old man had also been watching the sky. He and his sons were trying to get the animals aboard before the rain began. He was much too busy to notice when little Achbar slipped onto the back of an ostrich and nestled among the bird's tail feathers.

The soft feathers tickled Achbar's nose, and he nearly sneezed as the ostrich walked with its mate up the long gangplank and into the ark. But he had to be quiet and go unnoticed by the old man. Achbar had not been chosen—he was a stowaway!

"Achoo!"

Once aboard, Achbar sneezed so hard that he tumbled out of the ostrich's tail feathers and onto the hard wooden floor. The fall stunned him, but in a moment he was up and running for cover.

The air was filled with sounds of every description—the screeching of birds, the flapping of wings, barking and growling, and loud, terrifying roars. His instincts told him there was danger everywhere. Scurrying across the deck, he darted under the shell of a huge tortoise that was dozing beside its mate.

With all the creatures finally aboard, the old man and his sons
pulled the wooden doors shut against the coming downpour.

Suddenly, a great shock of thunder shook
the massive vessel, and the creatures all fell
silent. The *plip, plop* of the first drops of rain
could be heard striking the roof of the ark.

The rain poured down day and night and did not stop. Streams, rivers, and oceans overflowed. Soon villages were washed away, then towns and cities were drowned as the torrent increased. The water rose over the treetops, finally covering the peaks of the highest mountains.

The whole world was under water. Nothing could be seen above the terrible flood except the ark, pitching back and forth in the storm.

The animals crowded close together inside the ark, frightened
but snug and dry. Achbar was worried about being discovered by
the old man. He knew he didn't belong, so he moved from place

to place in search of a safe hiding spot among the other creatures.

As the waves lifted and tossed the ark, Achbar hid in a forest of elephant legs.

As the raging wind lashed the decks, Achbar hid high and dry in the mane of a seasick lion.

After ten days of rain, he hid with a pair of storks in a nest of twigs. Still the rain continued day and night.

After twenty days of lightning and thunder, Achbar tried
tucking himself into a rhino's ear. But he wasn't there long—
it was a very uncomfortable hiding place!

After thirty dark days, while the downpour continued, he burrowed in the folds of a sheep's warm, bushy wool. It was a snug place to hide, but the ram grew annoyed, so Achbar had to move on.

At last, the rain came to an end on the forty-first day. The ark drifted over the silent world. Long days passed slowly.

Then one day a great wind blew down from the sky. It rushed over the waters and began to dry all that it touched.

As the waters slowly receded, the ark came to rest on a lone

peak rising out of the ocean. The old man was hopeful. He believed it was a sign that they would survive.

Achbar was excited. Forgetting to hide, he raced out onto the deck. He leapt up onto the railing and peeked over the side. Where once he had seen nothing but ocean, now a craggy mountaintop appeared below him, reaching deep into the waters.

Achbar remembered he was a stowaway and scampered on top of a giraffe, hiding behind its horns. He watched the old man below release a dove. The dove flew from the ark, rising into the sky. Achbar watched her go until she was just a white dot on the horizon, surrounded by water in every direction.

The dove found no place to land. Water still covered the entire earth except for the peak they rested on. Exhausted, she finally returned to the ark.

Seven days passed, and the dove was again released. All day long the old man, his family, and the animals watched the sky and waited.

At dusk, the dove finally returned, with a sprig of fresh olive in her beak. The old man knew it meant the dove had found dry land! Surely it was only a matter of time before the waters subsided completely.

Soon, the mountaintop beneath the ark appeared to rise as the water gradually receded. They were safe now—the old man was sure. The animals, too, sensed that all would be well. They bellowed and roared and cackled and crowed while the water slowly went down.

Finally, the old man and his sons opened the doors and let down the gangplank. The creatures spilled out, covering the land in every direction.

Achbar just sat for a moment on firm ground. With the ark nearly empty, there was no reason to hide any longer. He looked all around and sniffed at the air. The earth had been washed clean.

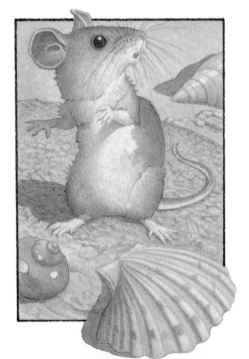

Achbar saw a family of mice leaving the ark. Just as he decided to follow along, he heard the old man's voice. "Go forth and prosper and lead righteous lives," he said to his sons and their wives.

"We were blessed from the very beginning," the old man said, looking up to the sky. At that moment, the sun lit the earth and a glorious rainbow appeared.

Achbar paused and looked at the old man, then at the sky, and was very happy.

Then the little stowaway scurried down the mountainside to
join the others of his kind in the brand-new world.